There Was an Old Woman Who Lived in a Book

Jomike Tejido

JIMMY PATTERSON BOOKS
LITTLE, BROWN AND COMPANY
NEW YORK   BOSTON   LONDON

Once upon a time there lived an old woman and her six children. One afternoon she called them in for supper, but no one came to the table.

She searched all their rooms.

She looked upstairs and downstairs, and checked their usual hiding spots.

I will find my missing kids!

The Old Woman hurried to her neighbors' house.

It was a long way to the farm. If she wanted to find her kids before nightfall, she needed help.

At the farm, they saw a boy climb down a giant beanstalk.

Along the way, they saw Cat, Spoon, Dog, and Cow, who was about to jump over the moon.

At the castle's entrance, a large egg sat on the wall.

Inside the castle, they met the princess.

In the garden, they climbed up a hill and found two children with a big pail of water.

They traveled through every book in the village on the bottom shelf.

No, they're not here. And
neither is a bundle of my sticks!

Finally, there was nowhere left to check but the Dark Woods.

The group walked on for several long pages, until they discovered a house covered in sugary treats. They stopped for a snack, and a witch rushed out the front door.

Wicked Witch, did my children come here for your treats?

They all held on to Papa Bear and set off.
Deep, deep into the book, they found the Big Bad Wolf's lair.

As the wolf scampered off, Humpty Dumpty spotted something strange among the twisty tree branches.

That night, everyone gathered in the Old Woman's book.
Even the Wicked Witch joined in. She brought the best desserts.

To Sophia and Fuji: Dream big. Don't quit. —*Pop*

Copyright © 2019 by Jomike Tejido

Hachette Book Group supports the right to free expression and the value of copyright.
The purpose of copyright is to encourage writers and artists to produce the creative works that enrich our culture.

The scanning, uploading, and distribution of this book without permission is a theft of the author's intellectual property.
If you would like permission to use material from the book (other than for review purposes),
please contact permissions@hbgusa.com. Thank you for your support of the author's rights.

JIMMY Patterson Books / Little, Brown and Company
Hachette Book Group
1290 Avenue of the Americas, New York, NY 10104
JimmyPatterson.org

First Edition: October 2019

JIMMY Patterson Books is an imprint of Little, Brown and Company, a division of Hachette Book Group, Inc.
The Little, Brown name and logo are trademarks of Hachette Book Group, Inc.
The JIMMY Patterson Books® name and logo are trademarks of JBP Business, LLC.

The publisher is not responsible for websites (or their content) that are not owned by the publisher.

The Hachette Speakers Bureau provides a wide range of authors for speaking events.
To find out more, go to hachettespeakersbureau.com or call (866) 376-6591.

ISBN 978-0-316-49305-5

LCCN 2019930697

10 9 8 7 6 5 4 3 2 1

PHX

Printed in the United States of America